How to Outsmart a

Vampire

Eric Braun

BLACK
RABBIT
BOOKS

Hi Jinx is published by Black Rabbit Books
P.O. Box 3263, Mankato, Minnesota, 56002.
www.blackrabbitbooks.com
Copyright © 2020 Black Rabbit Books

Jen Besel, editor; Michael Sellner, designer;
Omay Ayres, photo researcher

Library of Congress Cataloging-in-Publication Data
Names: Braun, Eric, 1971- author.
Title: How to outsmart a vampire / by Eric Braun.
Description: Mankato, Minnesota : Black Rabbit Books,
[2020] | Series: Hi Jinx. How to outsmart ... | Includes
bibliographical references and index.
Identifiers: LCCN 2018015178 (print) | LCCN 2018024012
(ebook) | ISBN 9781680729306 (e-book) |
ISBN 9781680729245 (library binding) | ISBN
9781644660621 (paperback)
Subjects: LCSH: Vampires—Juvenile humor. |
Wit and humor, Juvenile.
Classification: LCC PN6231.V27 (ebook) | LCC PN6231.V27 B73
2020 (print) | DDC 818/.602—dc23
LC record available at https://lccn.loc.gov/2018015178

Printed in China. 1/19

Image Credits

Contents

Chapter 1
They Vant to
Suck Your
Blood

Imagine this. It's the dead of night. The moon is bright. Trees cast creepy shadows across your room. A bat floats through your open window. Before your very eyes the bat changes into a person. The person smiles, sharp fangs gleaming in the moonlight.

Stop there before you wet your pants. This is just an *example* of a vampire **encounter**. But you know from movies you could meet a vampire at any time.

Prepare Yourself

Vampires are dangerous creatures. Stories say they are people who have died. Then they come back to life. They suck the blood of the living. So if you have blood, you need to know how to outsmart vampires.

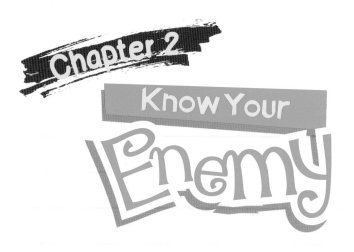

Chapter 2

Know Your Enemy

To outsmart vampires, you need to know about them. People have told vampire stories for hundreds of years. Not all stories describe the creatures the same way. But there are some signs to look for.

Vampires only come out at night. Daylight weakens or kills them. Did you see a guy sizzling in the sunlight? It could have been a vampire.

No Reflections or Shadows

Another good thing to know is that vampires don't cast shadows. And they can't check themselves out in mirrors either. They don't have **reflections**!

What they do have is super strength. They can lift 50 math books at once. Some can turn into bats.

Stories say vamps don't show up in photos, either. If someone avoids a selfie, be careful.

11

Chapter 3
Outsmarting a
Vampire

Now let's talk about stopping vamps. An old story says vampires have to count every grain of salt they see. If one is chasing you, throw a bunch of salt on the floor. The vampire will need hours to count all that salt!

Mirror, Mirror

Another **tactic** requires some preparation. Put lots of mirrors in a room. Make sure the mirrors reflect on other mirrors. Make it mirror madness. Then go in the room. When the vampire enters, he or she will see hundreds of you. But vampires don't have reflections. The only vamp you'll see is the real one.

Don't laugh at the confused vampire. He or she will hear you!

Cover the Smell

Vampires love human blood. They can smell it. You need to **disguise** the smell of your tasty blood. You could try rubbing garlic on your body. Putting rotten eggs in your pocket might help too.

Tip

Maybe use both garlic and rotten eggs for extra protection.

Trick 'Em

Here are a couple more ways to trick the undead. First, wear fake fangs. Then the vampire will think you're a vampire. Fangs also come in handy for eating apples.

Finally, carry an alarm clock. If a vampire comes around, set the alarm off. Stretch, yawn, and say, "Good morning!" He or she will be terrified of burning in the sun. The vampire will run to the safety of a dark coffin.

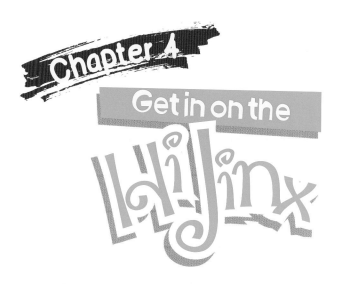

Chapter 4

Get in on the

Hi-Jinx

Of course, vampires are just story characters. But it is fun to think about defeating one in person.

Vampire stories might have started because of some real people. Vlad Dracula was a **cruel** ruler. He lived in Transylvania in the 1400s. He **impaled** his enemies on stakes. Then he ate dinner while they died. Stories say he dipped bread in their blood.

Don't try this yourself. That's gross.

Take It One Step More

1. Long ago, people believed in vampires. They used the stories to explain mysterious deaths. What's something people believe in today that might sound silly in the future?

2. Why do you think vampires are popular in books and movies today?

3. Research vampire bats. Why do you think they have vampire in their name?

GLOSSARY

cruel (KROOWL)—known to cause pain or suffering

disguise (dis-GYZ)—to change the usual appearance of someone or something so people won't recognize it

encounter (in-KAHWN-tur)—a meeting with something or someone

impale (im-PEYL)—to cause a pointed object to go into or through something or someone

reflection (ree-FLEK-shun)—an image seen in a mirror or shiny surface

tactic (TAK-tik)—a method for accomplishing something

BOOKS

Loh-Hagan, Virginia. *Vampires: Magic, Myth, and Mystery.* Magic, Myth, and Mystery. Ann Arbor, MI: Cherry Lake Publishing, 2017.

Shea, John. *Vlad the Impaler: Bloodthirsty Medieval Prince.* History's Most Murderous Villains. New York: Gareth Stevens Publishing, 2017.

Uhl, Xina M. *Vampires.* Strange … but True? Mankato, MN: Black Rabbit Books, 2018.

WEBSITES

Monster 101: All about Vampires
www.cbc.ca/kidscbc2/the-feed/monsters-101-all-about-vampires

Vampire History
www.history.com/topics/vampire-history

Vampire Scare Grips Europe
www.si.edu/object/yt_-Qb-J4tDECE

23

INDEX